The journey of the warrior Link Rider

Dedication:

Ito whom it may concern I would like to dedicate this to everyone who have helped me write this book thank you.

Prologue

We have to Alfred, we have to save this baby so he can one day rise and learn and defeat shadow he is our only hope. He has to live and survive even though he is the only survivor at least we saved one child. We have to send him to the human world called "Earth". Hurry up now, we have to quickly go through the dimension, wait which house do we bring him to? Just pick whichever says, Alden. Okay, hurry he's coming! Goodbye Rider, we'll surely meet again until the time comes, you will have to save us from "shadow". But for now, I bid you farewell. He rings the bell and someone comes and picks him up she reads the note: "please take care of this child, his name is Rider until the time comes, give him this note that is attached to this one, only he can see it so please don't read it. And thank you we live him in your hands. Alfred and Alden". Let's go". "Yes, yes open the portal". "Wait somebody's there", "who?". "I am not sure to hang on let me check". When Alfred goes to check in there that mysterious person was shadow, he takes out his sword and stabs it right through Alfred's heart but Alden escapes just in time shadow does not yet know where they have put rider in so he goes back to his dimension to this day Shadow is still looking for Rider so he can capture him and kill him then his goal would be set. Shadow was originally born in the place he destroyed, he was banished because he was trying to kill and overthrow the king but he was saved just in time by Alfred and Alden, so he claims revenge and he wants to kill every single person that was there. “One day, I swear one day I will get revenge!!”. (said Shadow). Now back to the women. “Dear come here there’s a baby on the mat”. “What? we'll check if there is anyone else outside”. She checks there is no one there. “Let’s adopt him he needs a home. “Ok”. Now these nice couples have been taking care of rider and they are his new family and he is now safe and sound for now. There is a force that is trying to find Rider, Shadow will be trying to find rider and either kill him or make him be the prisoners in his dungeon.

Chapter 1

"Hey rob what should we name him?". "Uh... how about Link?". "Why link?". "Well it said on his tag that his name is Link rider, so, I think we should just stick with that". "Ok, Link Rider it is". At ten years old, as link grew up not knowing his real parents he began to think a lot recently and that point he was getting a little confused. Until that day. "Hey Arthur?". "Yeah what is it Link?". "Do you think I am adopted I mean do you think my "mom" is not my mom? Tell the truth don't lie". "Ok, if you're telling me, to tell the truth, well then here it is, yes, you are adopted I knew and I just didn't tell you because I know you would be heartbroken". "So I am adopted well the who are my real parents?". "I don't know but they are your parents now and you should accept that fact because they are your parents now.

Chapter 2

(It has now been 10 years later.) Rider is now about to go to college and now his mom calls him. Rider, come on you're going to be late to school. "In a minute mom, I am coming". Okay. Did you do your homework? "YES". Okay come down and eat breakfast. "Okay coming". He comes down and just when he sits, out of nowhere he asks this bizarre question, "hey mom who are my real parents". (June told him that he was found on their doorstep and that she isn't his real mother. It took him a while to take that in and now it has been two months after). She wasn't saying anything for 10 minutes and then told him she will talk with him about that when she comes home from work. He said "fine" then left for school. When he goes to school he usually goes to his friends table and talks to them but today he didn't feel like it because he had a lot in his mind right now especially about finding about his parents or where he was born etc....... He then goes to his class, works, and then when school is finished he walks with his friends until he reaches his home. Today he did none of that because he wanted to get home early and wants to hear what she knows. He gets on his bike and says to his friends, "sorry guys, can't today got to go home early, see ya tomorrow". Then he leaves and petals his bike so fast that he makes it to his house in 17 minutes which is going to be a new record for him. On his way, he sees a mysterious man that is in need of help so he helps him and asks if there is anything he needs help with the man says something and then he leaves. After that rider realizes that he is going to be late so he gets there really fast so he still had the new record. When he gets to his house he suddenly remembers what the old man said: "thank you Link Rider we shall meet again along with your way on your journey". He repeatedly hears that on his head and he gets a big headache. He found that really odd and didn't know what that guy meant. He went to the kitchen and took a medicine that helps stop headaches. Before he goes up he realizes that he forgot to lock the door so now anyone can get in and as he tries to go lock it he sees the knob turning he is so scared that he runs off to his room. Now someone enters the house.

Chapter 3

Rider is still scared but then he hears a voice. “Rider I'm home”. Then he realizes it's his mom. “Hey, mom”. Then he remembers that she was going to tell him who his parents were and where he was born. Back to Rider. “So you are going to tell me what you know about my parents or where I came from?”. June: “yes that, well I don’t have much info and it’s because I didn’t get to see the person. They rang the bell and left. And then I found you…. But in the letter it said that there’s something attached to this and that I should give it to you when you are ready to learn about where you came from and who are your actual parents, oh and the person promised me to not read the attachment so, I kept my promise; Hang on let me go find it should be in the attic… let me go get it……” She goes to the attic and is searching through all the boxes. She couldn’t find and then at the last box she saw something…. “Aha found it, here it is, now rider I just want you to know I'll be there for you always and if you want to share what you read on that letter I am here”. “Okay. I should go to my room, then I'll read it. Thank you, mum”. Rider goes to his room, and then he reads the letter: “to Link Rider. You will read this when the time has come”. When he opens the letter he reads it and drops everything and leaves. The letter says: “Dear Rider, I know you have a lot you want to know about us and you, so I will tell you this right now you are the prince of our dimension we had to save you so we sent you to the mortal world called “Earth”. You and we have been targeted by this evil overlord named Shadow. He and his army forces almost wiped us out you were our only hope to surviving so you were the one and only one we had to save in order for you to save us. If you want to know more, come to this location----- warehouse 13, when you get there yell the word Alvador. This will trigger our dimension to open but be care full”. He didn’t tell his mom anything because it is just unbelievable and he didn’t believe it himself and he denied it and kept it a secret. Meanwhile, on somewhere off the map, there is a fortress and there is where Shadow is. "Sir! I have found evidence that Link Rider is indeed still in the human realm and I have located that he is in one of these houses". "Great work men now I don't have to kill you so where did you say he was?". "Um.... over there sir". "Okay, i need one of you to do it um you there". "Yes, sir". "Go and check through all of those homes and see if one of them knows Link Rider". "Yes, sir". "Uh, sir?". "What is it?!". "Um, there are tons of houses there I am not sure if we can find them still". "Okay I need two more to go with him and the first one to find him gets to be one of my henchmen's". "Yes, sir!". "I am going to be the first". "No, I am". "No, I am!". And so they go and meanwhile on the other-other side there is a mysterious man over there. "(Gasps) Rider it’s you I have to go now!". "No, you can't if you go now with your condition you will never be able to get your injuries healed again!". "No I have to it is Rider I have finally found him at last!". As this mysterious fellow has said he needs to see Rider but is he a good guy? And also on the other side as well there lies this old man. "It will be soon that you and I meet again link rider until that day comes I will stay here in this dimension". Now back to Rider. Rider is still confused and doesn't know if that letter is a prank or not, so he forgets about it but will still be in memory so what will he do?...... as he comes down the stairs, he sees his mom waiting for his response...

Chapter 4

So, what happened Rider? "nothing mom". Okay. Wait are you sure because you look a little confused". It's nothing mom don't worry about it. "Alright, come on you have to go to school, if you don't leave in 10 minutes, you will be late again. Now hurry up and eat breakfast I made eggs and bacon and toast and your favorite drink orange juice". "Okay". He sits down and eats the breakfast. "Thanks, mom bye now I've got to go now". On his way to school he meets up with his friends but he mostly talks to his best friend Arthur. "Hey, buddy what's up?". Nothing much. "Okay". Wait who's that? "Who that? dude, he's our teacher, you remember him right he's our home Ec teacher". I'm pretty sure I've never seen him before. Umm... I'm going to talk to him. "Okay". Umm, excuse me sir? "yes?" "what is it?" umm… do I know you from somewhere umm… Alfred, Alden… (the teacher says it in his mind), ("… It's him it's the survivor, I should go tell lord shadow, then he might promote me for finding him!".) "no I am sorry young man but I have not heard of those names. Well, I should be on my way, and I will see you in home ec". Ok, thank you, sir. He goes back to Arthur. Well, that was weird. Hey, Arthur. "Ya?". I am pretty sure I've never met this guy until now. "What are you talking about? He's our home ec teacher remember?". Oh ya, now I remember! (he lied). "About time, so you okay?". Ya, why? "Well you did seem pretty down today, what were you thinking". Oh, nothing just stuffs. "Okay but if you really want to tell me what's on your mind just say so I am right here". "Okay". After school ended Arthur and Rider were both walking home when they meet their Home Ec teacher suddenly. "Oh hello, there you two, fancy meeting you here". "Yes sir, what a coincidence". "So where are you boys heading?". "Home". "Great". "Great what sir?". "Great that only you two are here". Why is that great sir? "It's great because then I can capture one of your friends Young Prince of Alvador!". The teacher grabs Arthur and is flying floating away. "Wait what's happening?! Rider help!". Arthur!!!!! Nooooooo! "If you want your friend back and your mother you have to come with me! Link Rider!". Wait he also has my mother! I have to go home now! He arrives at his house only to see his door left opened, his house trashed, and he couldn't find his mother! she was gone! He remembered what the letter had said: If you want to know more, come to warehouse 13 and shout the word Alvador……. He ran as fast as he could and made it to warehouse 13. It was shady looking and almost torn down. He realized it was abandoned, so that causes him fewer worries about getting into trouble. He shouted out the word~ "ALVADOR!". He saw a light or something opening and then someone or something came out of a Dimension portal. Rider was stunned, it was the same old man he helped when he was going home yesterday!

Chapter 5

It's you! The man I saw yesterday! Why are you here! "I am here because you called me here, Link Rider". Again he remembers what that man said to him before he left "Link Rider we shall meet again along the way on your journey". How do you know my name?! "I know because I know Alden and Alfred Alden was captured and was killed by one of Shadow's men and Alfred is somewhere unknown we don't know where he is nor is he alive". Take me to where Shadow is now! I need to save my friend and mother! "You can't … you are not strong enough nor you are ready!". Then train me and teach me how to defeat him! "What you think it's easy? Just like that? Ha! You must be a fool! You can never beat shadow with that attitude! I can only help you with what I can do and what I can do is guide you to your journey I cannot train you but you might find someone that can. I will take you there if you're willing". I will go with you. Whatever it takes I will risk it. "Great buckle up we are going". Wait for what? whoa!! What was that! "We are here the "Milky way trance". Why are we here? What is this place? For you to find a trainer of course. Oh and this place is really crowded and has some dangerous people so be CAREFUL". Okay, who are we even looking for? "we are looking for Dagger". Who? "Dagger he used to be a very powerful warrior back, but he retired for some reason and just vanished but I managed to track him down". Okay, but what makes you think he'll help us and train me? "He will when he hears the word Shadow when shadow attacked his home Dagger came fist to fist with him he lost but he was the first to getting really close to him and almost defeating him so I think he is the right person to be your trainer. Let's go talk to him". Excuse me, sir, we were wondering if you were Dagger? "shh. kid don't say my name!" "What do you want?". Well, I was wondering if you could train me. (the old man) "really just like that, you asked him to train you?". As I was saying can you train and help to defeat Shadow? "Shadow?! Ha! You?!! Listen, kid, you need to be at least another millennium old to at least look at his face! What makes you think you've got what it takes!". It's because I know I can defeat him! and save my mom and best friend! So please train me if not I'll get a new trainer and just so you know he's the one who wanted to make you be my trainer! "Oh, and who's that?" "Uh, hey Dagger it's been awhile since I've seen you how's it going, old friend". " Alfre-". Arc signals him to not say his name. "Uh I mean Arc Drane! You're alive!". "Shhhh… come on now don't expose me!". "Hey kid I accept, I'll train you but you have to show for it we'll first have to go to a deserted island or something to practice full strength and hidden away from others". "Got that covered our best destination would be the andromeda island only a few know about it but no has gone there because they want to be safe but my calculations say it exists and we could teleport there with my wormhole opener", said Arc. "Okay get ready cause it's time for training I am not going to lie to you, it will be hard kid so get ready!!". Okay and thank you very much, sir.

<u>Chapter6</u>

Meanwhile, at Shadow's Fortress.... He he he I am surely going to get a promotion now heeeeehheehhe! Arthur: "Let me out!!!!!! Rider Helpppppp!!!!!". "No one is here to help you boy you are our bait and prisoner ha ha hahaha!~". "Sir" I have also brought this woman I think she is his guardian, he will surely come now for sure!". " Ms. Jane! Are you okay?!". "Arthur! Why are you here?! Have you been captured too?". "Yes I believe so, I don't know why for some reason this guy captured me and kidnapped me! He said something about Rider having to come here to save me or something like that". "Oh my, what have Rider gotten himself into? Well at first of all I hope he's okay". " Yeah, me too". " lord Shadow am I getting promoted? Am I ????". "Yes, Dunfrey but I asked you to bring the boy not these people". "Well sir, they are close to him so I thought if I would take them he will surely accept the offer and try to come here which our trap will be upon". "Oh then excellent so are you sure it's him? the survivor?. "I am absolutely certain that that is him, sir". "Okay if you say so". "Help get us out". "Get us out!!!". "Quiet human just shut up and stay there and we won't do anything else to you if you behave". "Wouldn't count on it". "Quiet!". Now back to Rider~. What do we do first?. Dagger: "well let's see here you have to have a strong body so the first part of training! get all these metals and heavy items to the other side of the shore". Whhaaaat!!! I can't do that!. " exactly so you have to go smallest to biggest okay come let's go training starts in 3-2-1 GO!". That will keep him occupied and he is still training, so Arc, how are you still alive I saw you die right there in front of my eyes". "Sorry can't tell you, so what have you been doing all these days?". " Nothing, just doing stuff". "So you gonna tell that kid that you're really Alden?". "DON'T TELL HIM!". "Sure but I am pretty sure he might find out by himself". "Wait how did you know that he is the survivor that Alfred and I saved?!". "I didn't but thanks for telling me haha". "Wait for what?!!!, well don't tell him or anyone about this conversation". "Okay". "Hey Rider, that's enough for today, you can rest now, but you have to get up early tomorrow to get the rest of this to the other side after that you have to go underwater and search for a hermit crab and they blend in the ocean pretty well so let's see if you can actually do it". "Okay I'll try but don't expect me to finish it". "Okay time for dinner eat up because you won't get to eat anything else until you finish putting those on the other side". Okay. "now go to sleep early". Okay. "When are you actually going to train him?". "This is training". "Come on I know well enough to know what you're doing and what you're thinking". "Oh really now, what am I thinking now?". "I don't know what you're thinking right now but I know you well enough to at least know what you're thinking or what you were going to". "Okay the truth of the matter is I am not sure if he's the right person to be my successor, he's not ready yet he has a lot to know and face the enemy ". "Oh come on he's ready he is the only one capable of defeating shadow I know I'm taking a long shot but I believe he is the one to get revenge for my people". "Let's see if he is ready or not and don't jump to conclusions". "Okay, but I still don't think he's ready but if you say so I'll give him a chance, you do know that what I'm making him do for his training isn't even the tip of the iceberg right?". "Yes, i know". "After all we did train together with master". "Yes, the good old days well until shadow came and that our master gave his life to save us and that's why I've been targeting shadow, trying to know where he is". "Well you're in luck I do know where he is and I know where he will be moving to next". "How do you know all that stuff?". "Well he did kill my master as well as destroying my home so I guess we're in the same boat, and I can't tell you where I got it from but I can tell you that there's a spy there working for me". "nice". "Just kidding I got it from some of the people that survived from shadow's

destruction when he invaded their homes and destroyed their city or was it the town? I am not sure but I know where he is so that's a win for us". "Yes it is, so what should we make him do next.

For his training?". "Oh I know, remember when master used to train us? you know what he made us do when we told him to train us?". "Oh, that ha nice okay time to get serious". "Hey, kid come over here". Yes? "This is what I want you to do next, I am going to give you a rice, a single grain of rice you're going to write your goal in it and then give it to me got it?". Okay. Done. "That was fast, okay now I am going to throw it and you have to find it". What? I can't do that! "You want to defeat shadow and get strong don't you?". Yes, I guess so okay fine throw it. " okay, now go find it and remember to find it you have to clear your mind and only think about finding that single grain, got it?". Yes. "now go!". Now back to Shadow's fortress: "hey you there, what's going on?". "Oh sir, um, well, we have recently found out that someone from here is a spy for the enemy". "What who is it?!", "we don't know yet sir". "Immediately, go find the spy and bring him to me!". "Yes, sir". "Now, where are the prisoners?". "There in the dungeon cell sir you can go there right now the elevator is ready". "Thank you now, let's go".

Part two of the book

Ok so so far in the book, there is a kid named Rider who was a normal boy so he thought until this imposter of his home ec teacher captured his friend and mother. And now he has to go and save them along with his way he meets this old man who is named "Arc" but later found out that "Arc is really Alden. Arc finds him a trainer and his name is Dagger he is fierce he has an X mark on his eye which shows he survived shadow. Shadow is the villain he has ordered his men to go find rider and when one of his subordinates found him that person took what was closest to him his mom and best friend Arthur now he has ventured off to go save them and defeat shadow. Rider asks dagger to train him and at first, he said ok but he wasn't actually training him. Now we're here where rider has to find this one single piece of rice that has been thrown in the sandy desert~~~~~~~

Chapter 1

Now back to Rider……. Aha I found it!!!!!!!!! And who said it was hard?! "Um, it was you kid". Oh yeah, well never mind that I found it! "Ok now on to the next one, Arc, take us to the Milky Way Trance again". "Okay". They arrive there and this is what Dagger does, "okay kid, I am going to put you in a tournament, you are going to have to beat people that are 10x your strength and ability so good luck". Ha, this will be easy watch me beat them who's my first opponent, "nope it's opponents". No worries I can still beat these weaklings. "Okay, good luck". The moment rider went up there and when the referee said go they wiped him up with one single blow, everyone started laughing at him so did his "comrades", now this is what he's thinking: "why did I even think I can beat those guys I literally embarrassed myself and my master, I am nothing! I don't even know why I thought I could defeat shadow he has my mom and my best friend locked in his prison and all I have been doing was nothing!!!!! I AM A FAILURE! I COULDN'T DO ANYTHING! I am going to get stronger! To defeat shadow and to save them, my mom and my best friend I will do whatever it takes to save them! Now he is going to tell Dagger something important. Dagger, I don't care if you are actually training me or not I just want to get stronger! So please I want to learn more! "Alright, kid, I will but get ready to face the harshest training ever". "Here, take this sword". Wait, where did you get this? "Well when you were fighting I just saw it there and I took it simple as that". "Okay, I am going to show you how to properly use and defend with your sword, oh and these are the real deals so don't try to touch the pointy top or you're going to bleed a lot!". Seriously you are giving me a dangerous weapon? "Yeah but don't go showing it off or you're going to get in big trouble and I will have to pay for it!". "Now Dagger, you are going to have to be nice this young man". "Shut up Arc!". "Who's Arc? Oh, you mean this guy". "What!". He turns around and its Crafter, shadow's right-hand man he is equal in strength and intelligence with shadow but Shadow is a little stronger and smarter than Crafter but Shadow doesn't know what his motives are for joining shadow. "Crafter! how did you get here! how did you find us???!!!". "Hey now, that's not how you greet an old friend Dagger". "Shut up you are no longer our friend!!! You betrayed us and joined the dark forces and the worst part is you joined Shadow and destroyed tons of homes and cities! You have no right to be called our friend!". "Hey now, I've only come here to tell the young prince that we have his precious mother and friend in our dungeon and if he wants them back, to come to this location, that's all bye now". "Wait how do you know?!! Crafter tell me!!!!!". Wait what did he mean by young prince? Wait am I a prince?!. "Well I guess the cat's out of the bag, yes, Rider, you are a prince, a fallen prince because nobody really knows you are alive and nobody will know because they are dead, they've been wiped out by Shadow and you're the only survivor". What about Alfred and Alden?. "Well they are not here with us anymore I don't know much else but they are probably dead as well". What HE also killed them!!!! That is it! I am going to stop shadow! I will KILL HIM!!!!!!!!!!!!!!!!!. "Now now Rider you have to defeat him not kill him". But HE!!. "he killed and destroyed thousands of people if you kill him you would have stood to his level you would have become evil just like him, you would've become him!!!!!". Okay, i won't kill him, just defeat him and save my mom and best friend!!. "Now that's more like it now get out your sword, hold it up words, now, come attack me head on, I want to see how powerful your attack is". Okay, but I'm warning you if you get hit….. "Not to worry I won't get hit". Well, you seem pretty confident and just by that, I will beat you with one attack. "One attack? okay, let's see your skills "young prince". Here I come ha!!!!!!!!!!!!. "Too predictable". Wait what you're not gonna move? ha! this will be easy, wait where did you go?!. "Right here". Wait what Now!!!!!!!!!. How did you!!. "I know just more than wielding a sword or fight you know". Please! Teach me that move!. "I can't teach you unless you teach yourself". Ugh, stop with the wisdom words. "Those aren't, oh yeah, never mind". So shall we start master? "Master? Ha, I kinda like that name okay let's start training!". Okay, let's go!. They start training and then one day rider unlocked a hidden power that was deep within him, so now he is ready and fully trained, he has a secret weapon that will be waiting for Shadow now it's time for them to go find and defeat shadow.

Chapter 2

Back to Shadow's fortress: "I can't stand him!. That is it! I am going to get Shadow in trouble. He has a superior and he isn't that powerful. Once I free those prisoners and then tell lord Archer that shadow released the prisoners and now the prince won't come here, ooh, this is going to be good. After he dismisses shadow, I will take up the lead to become the leader, after all, I was meant to be the leader not him!!!". I've waiting so long for this opportunity to get shadow killed and fired haha this is surely going to go my way!". Crane came down the dungeon when no one was there and he then came to Arthur and rider's mom and said: "you are free now, you can go". "Hurry Mrs. jane, we've got to escape before they find us!". "Okay let's go! And thank young kind, sir". "Ya ya go!". "He he, they really thought they were free! Ha they are not that smart are they". "Ok, now I'm going to call Archer". He called Archer and told him that shadow released the prisoners. Archer came right away and called Shadow. "Shadow did you release the prisoners?!!!". "No sir of course not! That's ludicrous!!! I would never do such thing!". "Yet you destroyed tons of people's homes and cities". "Shut up Krane it's because I was told to I always follow command no matter what!!!". "Ok then let me show you what happened, the prisoners escaped and it is all your fault because they were in the dungeon on your behalf and you had the key prove that!". "I don't have the key! You do I am the one who instructed you to keep the key you're the only one that could've done it!". "Wait I didn't do it! Sir, you have to believe me!". "Shadow you have powers to see what people did right you can look into their memories right?". "Yes". ok, so do it at home let's see what he says is true or false oh and Krane was it?, if you lied to me and if we find out you are the one who freed the prisoners you bet that i will kill you i would dismiss you but you know a lot of information from us so good luck!". "Ok hey! He did do it! Krane, you will die!!!!!". "Great job shadow, now Krane time to say goodbye". "Wait, please sir, it's a frame he framed me!". "I did not! Here". He transplanted the memory to Archer and now Mr. jealousy, Krane, he is now dead.

Chapter 3

Back to Rider. Hey Dagger, "yes what is it?". I was wondering is arc ok?. "Yes why?". well he did get a surprise attack and got hurt. "Hey Ald~ i mean Arc you ok?". "Yes, what is it?". "Nothing just asking". "Wait, stop". "What is it?". "Someone is following us". "Hey whoever it is come out we know you're there!". "Oh dang it how did you find us". Wait i know that voice it's~". "Sorry pal but i can't have you telling them who i am". Alden no!!!. What did you do that for jerk!. "Ha ha, after all these years you haven't changed Alfred". "Oh come on i just told you not to tell them who i am". Wait Alfred?. (gasps) Alfred! It's me! Rider Link Rider!. "Wait Rider? Alden why is he here?". "ah , you weren't supposed to tell him that i am alden!!". "Oops sorry". Wait Alfred and Alden! It's you you guys are the ones who saved me from shadow! But i thought you died!. "Did you seriously tell him everything?!". "No, he came on his own to defeat shadow, shadow has captured his "mom" and his friend and he wants to go save him, wait, how are you still alive! I thought you were dead!". "Well not quiet, shadow did stab me but not through the heart, when you left and then shadow left i woke up in a hospital, then they had to do surgery to me and save me. After that I hid in silence and I've been looking for you two. Then I heard that some kid was fighting in a tournament and when I went there it was over but people were laughing so asked why and they told me and they said that there was 2 guys with him a one that's old looking and won that looks like it ate a dragon. I immediately new it was Alden that was there so that's how I found you"."then this guy told me that you guys went that way so he told me the directions and then i followed you guys up until now so how did you find rider?. "well it was back in the mortal world i was walking somewhere and i got this feeling that it was rider and when he helped me he told me his name and i was sure it was him. "ok and then what happened?. "well his mom and friend was captured by one of shadows men and so now rider has to go and find them and defeat shadow". "what else happened?". "well the reason why they found rider and how they captured his loved ones i don't know, rider would you tell us what happened?". well it all started when i went to school., i met up with my friend and i saw a teacher that i didn't now i thought he was new but arthur said that he was our home ec teacher and that he wasn't new t0o the school he was already here for at least 2 years. when i walked you to him i asked him if i knew him i remember the words alfred and alden and so i accidently said it out loud and for some strange reason he gasped then he said he didn't know anything so i thought it was weird but i didn't check up on it "oh so that teacher was one of shadow's minions ?". yes i think so. "ok then what happened?". well after that i went home wAlking with my friend and we saw our home ec teacher again swe accidently bumped into him then he said it is a coincidence meeting you here then we thought it was strange because all the teachers go the opposite way and we realized it before it was too late that our teacher was following us he captured arthur and said if i ever want him and my mum back i have to go find them. when i got home i remembered what the letter said it said tha5 if you want to learn more come to warehouse 13 and so i went there and i said the words i don't really remember then i saw someone coming out of a portal or something and it was alsac i mean alden. that's how all this happened. "Ok did you do your training?". Yes, but i still can't believe you are alive especially alden i mean arc he was with me the whole time!. "well we had to hide ourselves so nobody of shadow's men would track us down we didn't want people to find out the we were alive or the people would die they would be in trouble because of us". "so alden and alfred why and how did you find rider?". "well for our story, we knew that it has been 14 years and we knew that noe rider would ask about his parents so we can there right away for before 15 years we came 1 year ago. " Ok so but how did you track me down?. "well we had a photographic memory of where we send you to so it was easy for us to keep in check. "So I was checking at your school and Alfred was checking at your home so nothing bad happens and so i can find you. But one time a stranger came to your house i thought it was a guest so i didn't pay any attention to it. But as i turned my back that person took your mother so it was my fault. Can forgive Mr rider i am really sorry.. i tried to stop them but i was too late". It's okay now, we are here to help you and stop him once and for all!!. Now back to Shadow's fortress ; "No. no sir please forgive me, I just wanted to be the leader I hated that Shadow was the leader and not me! please don't kill me! please forgive me!". "i am sorry but it is too lAte you will have to die now". bring him, to the executioner place shadow". "yes sir!". you shouldn't have tried to destroy me krane no one can o dt hart to me! ha! now you will have to pay the price!". ha ha ha!!!!!!! now good bye! no, goodbye forever hahaha!". "no please ah, it was just a joke please forgive me". "nope"."goodbye forever crane, now i don't need an obstacle in my path hahah!". " now i won't miss you hahaha!".

Chapter 4

back to rider: "hey rider what else did you do during your training ?". well i don't know can't remember what was it that i was doing? oh dang it! i forgot!!. a person and comes out. "hello there would you please tell me where alfred is?". "no sorry sir but he is dead". "thank you i have everything i need now". ah sir?, you are floating. "whatever do you mean i am a sorcerer of course i can float!". "now which one of you is rider link link rider?". "no sorry you have the wrong people and who is this link rider?". "is he an escapee or something?". "yes the".so are you sure that he isn't here? no i don't know this link rider what is he a 15 year old who ran away and you're trying to capture him?. "no of course not link rider". yeah so?!. oh oh, oops. "thank you i knew it was you!. "i have come here to give his a message". "are you on the shadow side or good?". "good". "ok tell us your business here". "well i have come here to come and tell you that your mother and friend have escaped and they are on the run". how do you know that?!."simple i am the spy shadows fortress it was actually simply easy to infiltrate that to be honest i am too highly unmatched there's nothing i can infiltrate on". "i have come to warn you that he will come.". "who ? ". "he who is the strongest bounty hunter. "that guy why?!!". "he has been tasked to find rider either dead or alive". "so now there is someone else trying to catch me?!. "yes but you have to hide no matter how you view yourself you are not strong enough to defeat that guy he is on a slightly different level". but i have to atleast try!!!!. "okay but i warned you he is incredibly strong and powerful; rumors say that he has defeated the infamous Archer game who is thought to be t one of the this continent!!". "really? are you sure?!~". "yes until then i will have to go now or shadow will get suspicious of me and figure out i am the infiltrator they are looking for". Ok thank you very much we bid you farewell and good luck mister, mister?. "James, James Carles". "We will see you later sir and thank you again". Now James left and now rider is going to talk. Hey my mum and friend escaped we should go find them!. "I am terribly sorry but no, we can't go back after all this". Why not we can go and get them to safety!."if you go now Shadow will send one of his minions to go fetch them but if you stop him now, he won't be able to attack them listen to me Link rider!".

Chapter 5

"you have to defeat shadow now or never because once you go back he will come and find you again and he will destroy this universal dimension as well to find you!". i know that but they are free i want to go see them!!!. "right now your only objective should be trying to find shadow and defeat him!~". "link Rider you are our only hope!". no i am not we have dagger here!. "dagger can't fight shadow anymore last time dd that his arm was cut off". what you're lying he has a arm right there!. "actually i am, really good at hiding something and making it real, but ya, i lost one arm and that arm was my most powerful one with out that i will never be able to fight again so listen to them listen to us!". "you have to go and defeat Shadow!!". OK FINE LET'S GET MOVING. As they had for shadows fortress they have to find an alternate route because the original one has his minions all over just in case an intruder tries to get in. When they get in there was an alarm sound when alden accidentally touched the invisible laser. "really Alden! Come on". "Sorry but it was AN ACCIDENT ANYONE OF US COULD HAVE DONE IT SO PLEASE DON'T BLAME ME!"."LET'S HURRY!!!!". "BEFORE WE GET CAUGHT!". LET'S GO!. "WAIT THERE'S A PERSON HERE. "WHY HELLO THERE IF YOU WANT TO GO MEET SHADOW YOU HAVE TO GO THROUGH ME BUT IT WON'T BE A SURPRISE IF I COULD BEAT YOU. YOU HAVE TO STOP ME BEFORE YOU CAN EVER TRY TO DEFEAT MASTER SHADOW". IN UNISON. "AND US TOO!". "oh you guys are here you know i can do this

by myself you know you guys are not even qualified to be soldiers". "shut up we are and we will be soldiers we might also get promoted for doing this so then we can get a higher position than you!". "is that so, well i think you should just die right here". "wait wha~". "why did you do that to your own men?!". "because they were annoying of course what else do you need?"". "well first of all~". "no don't bother alfred". he is doing this his way and we'll do it your way". "ok who is going to fight him first?". i will go. "no rider you have to conserve your strength. to defeat shadow!~ go on, i will battle this one":., "be my guest all though i don't think you will beat me in 5 minutes". "what?!". "give me 5 minutes when it's over you have either lost or have been dead by my hands! ha ha, this going to be fun!". "let's see 5 minutes huh?, i am going to LAST MORE THAN 5 MINUTES HOW ABOUT THAT?!". "HA! NO ONE HAS LASTED THAT LONG BATTLING ME! YOU WILL LOSE RIGHT HERE AND NOW!". "OK BUT YOUR WORDS NOT MINE HA!". HE CHARGES HIS SWORD REALLY FAST AND SINCE HE HAD EXPERIENCE HE DEFEATED THE BAD GUY IN ONE STRIKE. "WHAT HOW CAN THIS BE? YOU MADE A HOLE THROUGH MY CHEST? NO YOU CAN'T DEFEAT ME!~ NO ONE CAN, YOU DID NOT DEFEAT ME!! NOT YET!". "I AM SORRY BUT YOU ARE JUST TALK AND NO ACTION TRAIN YOURSELF HARDER ON THE OTHER SIDE".
"NOOOOOOOOOOooo!!!!!!". "HA THAT WAS A COOL LINE I SHOULD REMEMBER THAT

ONE. NOW I SHOULD GO MEET UP WITH THEM SO OFF I GO". "WAIT! I AM NOT DONE YET ". "I AM SORRY BUT YOU HAVE LOST". "NOT YET HAAAAAA!!!!!!". "WAIT IS THAT A BOMB? YOU FOOL YOU'LL KILL YOURSELF ALOng WITH ME!". "I HAVE NEVER LOST And i will never will ha!!!!". "ok stop". "sheesh this guy is too crazy". "ok so i take this bomb and put it in the water and ok resume~". "haaa!! wait what where's my bomb??!!!". "why it's in the wATER OVER THERE WHY FOR?". "WHAT THIS CAN'T BE??!!!". "IT CAN'T BE". "WHO ARE YOU?!". (GASPS) "ALFRED". YOU IT'S YOU !!!!!!!. HOW ARE YOU STILL ALIVE! I THOUGHT MASTER SHADOW KILLED YOU!?!". "ACTUALLY THE OPPOSITE, I SURVIVED". "NO WHAT!? NO ONE CAN SURVIVE FROM MASTER SHADOW'S ATTACKS!~". THE ENEMY FALLS TO THE GROUND AND ALFRED HAS BECOME THE VICTOR . nOW BACK TO RIDER, DAGGER, AND ALDEN. I HOPE ALFRED IS OK. "DON'T WORRY, ALFRED IS STRONGER THAN HE LOOKS YOU KNOW HE COULD EVEN BE A LITTLE BIT STRONGER THAN DAGGER". "WELL NOT REALLY, HE'S NOT AS STRONG AS ME". "OK OK NOW LET'S HURRY UP! WE HAVE TO GO FIND SHADOW AND STOP THIS ONCE AND FOR all!!". the two in unison:" "ya!!". "hey there is another guy here." hello~". "ha! move out of our way". "nooo!!!!!". that guy flys off. "seriously is shadow that desperate now that he is just getting any random person on to be one of his soldiers". "probably but he is one that should be dealt with carefulness or otherwise if you overestimate him he will kill you in an instance!". " but if you do not and he overestimates you, you will be the clear victor here so good luck rider and don't overestimate him! all your training has come to this point now show him your power and defeat him!". ok. "our lives and every single beings life is now on your hands rider. Now go RIDER go! Every ones life and homes are in your hands rider now go! go and defeat him!". ok!!!!!!!!!. rider con nes in to to the fortress he sees shadow just standing there."hello rider i have been waiting so long no w how old are you now? 14? 15?". 15. i have come to defeat you shadow. "why are you calling me by that name? what happened to father?". what!!. "yes rider i am your father!!".noooo!!!!!!!!!!!. "Just kidding can't believe you fell for that". Shadow tried to be funny it turned out to be an epic fail. SHADOW the time has come i will defeat you!. "come on you don't even have a chance kid".

Chapter 6

now back to the others:" hey guys what's that over there?". "over where?". "over there!". "we don't know why you asking us?!". "hurry let's go there and check it out". "ok!". they walk in and they see these blueprints. "hey guys these are blueprints!". "what?!. "what's it about or what does it say?". "it's a doomsday device!!!". "what!!???". "let me see!". "her's right it is a doomsday device!!". "but who would?~". "SHADOW!!!!!!!". "i know he is an evil guy but never thought~". "a bAd guy will always be a bad guy". "we should go show this to rider!". "we can't!". "why not?!". "because~ he's off to fight shadow and if we show this to rider in front of shadow, shadow will kill us all because we saw his plans!!". "ok but what should we~". "well well well, what do we have here?, a couple of rats that shouldn't be here that are snooping around you know you should really put the "rats down". so they can never snoop or get up again". "who are you?". "me, i am just one of the eight generals who have come to see what all the commotion is about that's all". "wait you're one of the eight generals?!". ha! just kidding but you guys would be no problem to deal with judging that you two are old timers and the other one is just putting up the tough guy act. tell you what, i will let you two old timers off the hook because i am so nice how about that?". "who do you think you're messing with kid?!". "kid! haha ok you had your chance now you will die~". dagger punches him in the stomach. "shut up kid". the two said "this is what an old timer can do~". they both kicked him in the place where it hurts and then alden took the blueprint and hid it in his pocket. "just in case". "they left to go see rider and on their way they saw another weirdo burt this one was different. he showed no talk and all action so they were on their guards. "this guy must be the leader or something of those pathetic soldiers because he is pretty strong". "ya, i know right this one is worth giving our all in to". "ok lets go!". their attacks didn't even scratch that guy!.alfred and alden were giving their all but dagger wasn't he didn't even fight for some reason he lost his will to fight. but then he snapped out of it and with 2-6 strikes he and and the others all together defeated him. "wow, i have never used this much power before to strike down an enemy". "i know, this is the first for me". "me too"". "well not for me, this is the second the first time i gave it my all was when i fought shadow". "i hope the kid has what it takes to defeat shadow if not this was all for nothing". "what do you mean you hope?!". "you don't believe that rider will defeat shadow??!!"."well kind of, he didn't actually get to get enough training". "what!!!".what do you mean?". "well during our training i only taught him sword moves the rest he would would sleep". "well i am not too sure about that<". "what do you mean?". "i have seen him staying up all night performing something but i was never sure what it was, either sleep walking or just getting up and going to the bathroom or something like that". "so he was training extra hard every day??!". "yes i think so". "i am so proud of him. you know i am thinking about making him my successor". "took you long enough, well he is your first student that you have trained so it is clear that he would have been your successor". "ya true but i was not sure about training him because i didn't think he was the "one"."ok ok let's hurry rider must be in trouble". as they had out they talk about all sorts of stuffs they actually had lots of time on their hands.while they were doing that rider was ready to fight shadow so let's hope rider defeats shadow. on the other note in a far away place there's a headquarters it is the place that has all the eight generals and their leader guard. they will be talking about shadow and if he should be removed from his place. "i think shadow has fallen, he used to destroy stuff that was his passion now he does none of that!". "ya i agree i think it is time shadow stooped down his position and give it to one of my subordinates his name is al, he is one of my strongest soldiers and he is stronger than shadow after all, shadow is the last of the generals and he is weak compared to us". "well just because he is weak doesn't mean he has what it takes". "you always take his side ranger i think we do not need to listen to you opinion about shadow". "everyone quiet the chair men is here to speak his mind~". "thank ant, now everyone i think it is time to think if shadow should be released of his command or he should be saved now i am the one who chooses no matter who thinks what and it is up to me so i think he should be released of his command". "what??!!, but sir, shadow has been a valuable asset to us we can't just~". "careful what you say or he will do the same to you". "now i know you may not be agreeing to me but it is my choice and i have made it so there will be no doubts or changes shadow is to be relieved of his position and outcasted and well, since he knows about us and everything else we will have to kill him". shadow does not know this yet but he will soon die without the execution part now back to rider and shadow.

Chapter 7

ha!!. "easy, i can block that with one hand and without using my powers!". what! you're bluffing. "am i come at me then". i will ha!!!. wait what! how did you block that? !. "like i told you i can block that with one hand! hahahah!". no way this cannot be happening he is way stronger than i expected i can't defeat him it's over for mr!. "no, rider you must not fall into the dark side noPo! you can do it! believe in yourself gooo!". what, wAIT ALFRED DAGGER ALDEN YOU'RE All alive you defeated them?. "yes we did". "what this is not right they were my finest soldiers! how can they have ;lost! noo!!". now you have no soldiers to protect you shadow so you can give now or die!. "i would die then to give up!". "suit yourself". let's defeat him together guys!. in unison: "right". ha!. ha!. ha!. Ha!. altogether they combine their attacks and strokes shadow as fast as they can. "no this caNNOT BE I AM SHADOW ONE OF THE GREAT GENERALS NO! THIS IS NOT OVER!!". "what!, how can this be! all out Attacks together didn't even make him go down this is not possible!". i will not suffer deg=feet until my last breATH I WILL FIGHT!!. "RIDER, yes we will fight! ha!". "fools it is useless and with this final strike you all have been dead!". "i will give you the count of three to surrender rider, 1~". no way we will ever surrender to you!. "2~". "never!!!. "3, times up grand archanime destroy!!!!". guys get behind me now!. "but~". now!. i haven't fully mastered it yet but there's one move that might work against shadow!. "ok, we will com=over you go!". ok i am going to sneak from behind. "ok,go!". "hey shadow, do you want to know something somebody's here that knows you really well". "what, dagger is he here?"."uh.. ya". "i am fight here shadow no i mean assilem my old friend now enemy". "oh it is you i thought i killed you already back there~". while shadows been distracted rider comes from behind and his sword was glowing blue and then he attacked shadow with it and it pierced through shadow's chest and then shadow didn't actually die. "wait, why isn't he dying?!". he isn't dying he is changing into good."what!!". this move i created, it makes all bad guys turn back to good, normal and they're memories go away of all the destruction and mayhem they've made. "wow and you didn't tell is that before?". well it wasn't perfected yet so i didn't want to give false hope." okay you've mastered it right?. not exactly, no. "then what's going to happen t0po shadow?. he either dies or ya that's it oh yeah, he either dies or explodes so i think we should hurry AND LEAVE BEFORE TIME RUNS OUT SO LET'S GOOOO~. AND AS THEY LEFT SHADOWS FORTRESS EXPLODED ALONG WITH SHADOW STUDYING. now they have finally gotten revenge, killed shadow and have defeated one of the great generals which later on would come back and haunt them because shadow did have a superior and i am sure he'd want to get revenge but let's not get that far ahead.shadow has been defeated ands it is time for rider to go to his mom and friend and erase their memory of this ever happened and it is also time for shadow to say goodbye to dagger alfred and alden. good bye alfred alden and dagger, i will never forget you and if you ever need my help again, you can always come to me ask me to help you. "thank rider but i think it is time for us to go on our separate ways for now until the time comes i will never forget you goodbye". "see ya later kid oh and here's a gift from mre don't open until you get home". thanks dagger and goodbye. "oh at last it is me, goodbye ride, you said if we ever need your help but if you ever need our help feel free to call us here's this". what is it?. "it is a magical phone well it is in a shape of an orb though, with this you can call us anytime and we will always be there to listen and help you out". thanks but what about the others?."don't worry, i've already given them theres so they will always be able to help you if you need it"."well goodbye rider have a safe journey back oh and i used my powers to bring your mom and friend to their appropriate homes i also erased their memories and i've fixed your house so your mother won't question you about anything". really?, thank you so much alfred you have been a really great help to me i owe you the rest of my life to you so thank you very much. "no problem we'll see you later my boy". and as they all said their goodbyes rider went back home but on his way he met some peculiar people. one of them was alley he is so tiny and rider has made friends with him and they have been going on there journey to get back home and alley has decided to stick with rider so now their friends. rider has made home with his new friend then rider introduces alley to his mom and his mom and she thinks it's a "figurine" so she let's him keep it. After that everything went back to normal his mom and his friends were safe and sound he goes to school he comes back does his homework. it all started to become his everyday life again. But there is another villain waiting there in the dark one that is a much powerful foe and force than shadow ever was. What will come next ?, will rider come back to his warrior ways. what do you think will happen next? what will have become of link rider? what will he do? will h go back will he go find his fellow worriers again or will rider ignore everything and leave it to destiny to figure it out..... THERE IS STILL A DARK FORCE COMING AND RIDER HAS TO BE CAREFUL BECAUSE YOU NEVER KNOW WHAT WILL HAPPEN IN THE FUTURE BECAUSE OF YOUR ACTIONS.

Epilogue

It has now been 20 years rider is now a father and has two children and a wife. But his life's journey will still be going on because there is still some dark forces left a they want vengeance and are trying to track down rider and destroy him once and for all with shadow's death in their minds they are really angry. "Sir I have finally tracked down link rider". "good job men now it is time for our revenge". Now rider may not have seeing this coming but now a great and powerful force have come to get revenge on link rider and dagger alden and alfred. Rider gets the news from alden that a dark force is on the move and are now coming and trying to find him (rider). So now rider and his family are on the hide and trying not to get caught. Rider heads off to go find dagger alden and aldred and trying to put all this whole thing to an end. Rider: "i will bring this to an end! I don't want my family to get captured again! It is time to put this thing to an end! Once and for all!". Back to the bad guys. "Sir I have found where link rider is and where his family is". "Ok get ready time for payback".

www.ingramcontent.com/pod-product-compliance
Ingram Content Group UK Ltd.
Pitfield, Milton Keynes, MK11 3LW, UK
UKHW041833200726
13854UKWH00003BA/1119

9 781365 983849